Max's Easter Surprise

Grosset & Dunlap

Based upon the animated series *Max & Ruby*, a Nelvana Limited production © 2002–2003.

Max & Ruby ™ and © Rosemary Wells. NELVANA™ Nelvana Limited. CORUS™ Corus Entertainment Inc.
All Rights Reserved. Used under license by Penguin Young Readers Group. Published in 2008 by
Grosset & Dunlap, a division of Penguin Young Readers Group, 345 Hudson Street, New York, New York 10014.
GROSSET & DUNLAP is a trademark of Penguin Group (USA) Inc. Printed in the U.S.A.

Library of Congress Control Number: 2007012930

ISBN 978-0-448-44783-4   10

Max played with his windup toys.
"Peep, peep," went his Easter chicks.
"Yap, yap," went his noisy puppy.
"Zoom, zoom," went his motorcycle.

"Max," said Max's sister, Ruby, "we are going to decorate Easter eggs."
"Parade," said Max.

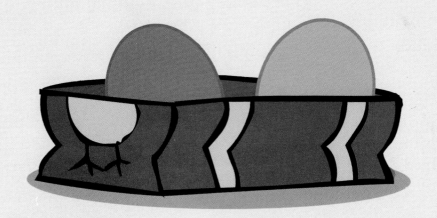

"No, Max," said Ruby. "Tomorrow is the Easter Parade."

"Today we decorate eggs," said Ruby's best friend, Louise.

"But you can help by carrying the eggs to the Easter basket," said Ruby.

Louise painted a beautiful green
egg and decorated it with pink lace.
"Here you go, Max," said Ruby. "Be
careful. Easter eggs break very easily."

But Max wanted a parade.
So he gave the egg to his chicks.

Ruby painted a blue egg with yellow spots.

"Parade!" said Max.

"The parade is tomorrow, Max," said Ruby. "Take the egg to the dining room and then come back for another one."

Max took the egg.
He gave it to his yap-yap puppy.

Ruby and Louise made eggs with macaroni faces.

"Grandma will love them!" said Ruby.

"Careful, Max!" said Louise. "Don't drop the eggs."

Max gave one egg to his big bad spider.
He gave the other egg to his motorcycle bunny.

Knock! Knock!
Grandma was at the door.
"Looks like you've been painting Easter eggs!" she said.
"They are all in the other room!" said Ruby.
"Let's go look," said Louise.

"Oh, no!" said Ruby. "Where are the eggs?"

Max's toys rattled and peeped and chattered and squeaked!
Each one was pushing an Easter egg.
"How wonderful," said Grandma.
"An Easter Parade!"